The Pride Street Crew

## 2

# Carrot Rap

Mike Wilson

*Published in association with*
The Basic Skills Agency

Hodder & Stoughton

**Acknowledgements**
*Cover: Stuart Williams/The Organisation.*
*Illustrations: Jim Eldridge.*

Orders: please contact Bookpoint Ltd, 39 Milton Park, Abingdon, Oxon OX14 4TD. Telephone: (44) 01235 400414, Fax: (44) 01235 400454. Lines are open from 9.00–6.00, Monday to Saturday, with a 24 hour message answering service. Email address: orders@bookpoint.co.uk

*British Library Cataloguing in Publication Data*
A catalogue record for this title is available from The British Library

ISBN 0 340 75306 4

First published 1999
Impression number    10 9 8 7 6 5 4 3 2 1
Year                 2004 2003 2002 2001 2000 1999

Typeset by Fakenham Photosetting Ltd, Fakenham, Norfolk
Printed in Great Britain for Hodder & Stoughton Educational, a division of Hodder Headline Plc, 338 Euston Road, London NW1 3BH by Athenaeum Press, Gateshead, Tyne & Wear.

JOHN / BONE

WESLEY / TALL

LUKE / SKY

SIMON / CUSTARD

CARL / SPOT

iii

Do you like music?
I do.
But not pop music.
Not bands with girls in.

I like rap music.
Hard and loud.
The rest of the Pride Street Crew
like rap music as well.

One time,
we had a go
at rap music.
We had a go
at rapping
with Wesley's Dad.
Wesley's Dad is a DJ.

One day,
a van stops
at Wesley's house.

'Hey Tall,' I ask.
'What's in the van?'
Tall says,
'It's a DJ rig.
It's my Dad's.'

We take a look.
The van is full of boxes.
Speaker boxes.
Lights. Everything.
It's mega!

We go with Tall's Dad.
We go to help him
set up the rig.

We help him try it out.
We take the van
to the church hall.
Tall's Dad sets up the wires.
He plugs in the record players.
Then he turns them on.

The record turns.
Tall's Dad drops the needle.

It's loud.
Drum and bass.
It's too much.
It makes your legs shake.
It makes your belly shake.
Custard puts his hands
over his ears.

I shout,
'You wimp Custard!'
But he can't hear.
The music is too loud.

Then Tall's Dad starts to rap.
He is so mega!
The words all come stabbing
out of his mouth.

The words are strong and angry.
He never slows down.
He never stops.

The Pride Street Crew
start to dance.
We dance all night.
Tall and Bone
and Spot and Custard and me.

Then we start trying to rap.
It's harder than you think.
But we have a great night!
Tall's Dad lets us have a go,
rapping into the mike!

So next day
I say to Wesley,
'Let's be rappers!
The Pride Street Crew!
We can be a wicked rapping crew!'

'But we got no DJ rig,' says Wesley.
'We need lights and sound
and a mike.
And records ...'

Trust Wesley.
Sometimes he can be so ...
normal.

No lights.
No problem, I say.

Custard finds a torch
in his Dad's shed.
Spot gets a desk lamp
from his house.
Now we have lights.
Sort of.

No mike.
No problem.

Bone goes home.
He's looking for a mike for us.
He comes back with ...
a carrot.
'What's that?' I ask.
'It's the best I can do ...'
says Bone.
He says the carrot
looks like a mike.
A bit.

It's all we've got.
We tie it to a broomstick.
Now we've got a mike on a stand.
Sort of.

No record player.
No problem.
In our loft,
there's an old record player.
I get it down.

It still works – just.
It's just a bit slow.

Now we're ready to rock!
But what are we going to rap
about?
Spot says:
'All the big name rappers,
they go on about guns,
and crime and stuff.'

I say,
'We can't do that.
We don't know about guns
and crime.'

Wesley says:
'You rap about your life.
You rap about the things you know.
The things you do.'

Custard says,
'What can we rap about?
Homework?
School dinners?'
He grabs the 'carrot-mike'
and begins to rap.

'We played a game of football
in the park.
We played and played
till it got dark.'

Hmmm.
Well, it was about our lives.
But it just wasn't very …
interesting.
Then I have a go.

'My Mum tells me
to tidy my room.
This mike is a carrot
tied to a broom!'

We all fall about.

Wesley laughs so much
he sits on the record player.
No more record player!
It didn't work that well, anyway.

We take it to the tip,
and throw it away.
We take the 'carrot-mike'.
We throw that away as well.

Custard takes his Dad's torch home.
Spot takes the desk lamp home.

Being a DJ was good fun
with Wesley's Dad.
But –
with a carrot and a broomstick
and a broken record player,
it just wasn't the same!

Two weeks later,
Dad is in the loft.
I hear him say to Mum,
'Where is my old record player?
Have you seen it?
It *was* up here in the loft ...'

I run for it.